THIS BOOK BELONGS TO:

....

....

EDWARD LEAR's
NONSENSE VERSE

Illustrated by Jonathan Bentley

ACC Children's Classics

ACC CHILDREN'S CLASSICS

an imprint of
Antique Collectors' Club Ltd, 5 Church Street, Woodbridge, Suffolk IP12 1DS, UK
and
Market Street Industrial Park, Wappingers' Falls, NY 12590, USA

Nonsense Verse first published 1999
Compiled by Amy McKay

ISBN 1 85149 704 8

British Library Cataloguing-in-Publication Data
A catalogue record for this book is available from the British Library

Published and printed in England
on Consort Royal Satin paper from Donside Mills, Aberdeen by Antique Collectors' Club Ltd.

CONTENTS

THE OWL AND THE PUSSY-CAT

The Owl and the Pussy-cat went to sea
In a beautiful pea-green boat,
They took some honey, and plenty of money,
Wrapped up in a five-pound note.
The Owl looked up to the stars above,
And sang to a small guitar,
'O lovely Pussy! O Pussy, my love,
What a beautiful Pussy you are,
    You are,
    You are!
What a beautiful Pussy you are!'

Pussy said to the Owl, 'You elegant fowl!
How charmingly sweet you sing!
O let us be married! too long we have tarried:
But what shall we d   for a ring?'
They sailed aw   year and a day,
To the lan   Bong-tree grows
And t̄   iggy-wig stood
w   his nose,

                              nose.

'Dear Pig, are you willing to sell for one shilling
Your ring?' Said the Piggy, 'I will.'
So they took it away, and were married next day
By the Turkey who lives on the hill.
They dined on mince, and slices of quince,
Which they ate with a runcible spoon;

And hand in hand, on the edge of the sand,
They danced by the light of the moon,
   The moon,
   The moon,
They danced by the light of the moon.

THE JUMBLIES

They went to sea in a Sieve, they did,
    In a Sieve they went to sea:
In spite of all their friends could say,
On a winter's morn, on a stormy day,
    In a Sieve they went to sea!
And when the Sieve turned round and round,
And every one cried, 'You'll all be drowned!'
They called aloud, 'Our Sieve ain't big,
But we don't care a button! we don't care a fig!
    In a Sieve we'll go to sea!'
       Far and few, far and few,
       Are the lands where the Jumblies live;
       Their heads are green, and their hands are blue,
       And they went to sea in a Sieve.

They sailed away in a Sieve, they did,
    In a Sieve they sailed so fast,
With only a beautiful pea-green veil
Tied with a riband by way of a sail,
    To a small tobacco-pipe mast;
And every one said, who saw them go,
'O won't they be soon upset, you know!
For the sky is dark, and the voyage is long,
And happen what may, it's extremely wrong
    In a Sieve to sail so fast!'
        Far and few, far and few,
        Are the lands where the Jumblies live;
        Their heads are green, and their hands are blue,
        And they went to sea in a Sieve.

The water it soon came in; it did,
 The water it soon came in;
So to keep them dry, they wrapped their feet
In a pinky paper all folded neat,
 And they fastened it down with a pin.
And they passed the night in a crockery-jar,
And each of them said, 'How wise we are!
Though the sky be dark, and the voyage be long,
Yet we never can think we were rash or wrong,
 While round in our Sieve we spin!'
  Far and few, far and few,
  Are the lands where the Jumblies live;
  Their heads are green, and their hands are blue,
  And they went to sea in a Sieve.

And all night long they sailed away;
 And when the sun went down,
They whistled and warbled a moony song
To the echoing sound of a coppery gong,
 In the shade of the mountains brown.
'O Timballo! How happy we are,
When we live in a sieve and a crockery-jar,
And all night long in the moonlight pale,
We sail away with a pea-green sail,
 In the shade of the mountains brown!'
  Far and few, far and few,
  Are the lands where the Jumblies live;
  Their heads are green, and their hands are blue,
  And they went to sea in a Sieve.

They sailed to the Western Sea, they did,
    To a land all covered with trees,
And they bought an Owl, and a useful Cart,
And a pound of Rice, and a Cranberry Tart,
    And a hive of silvery Bees.
And they bought a Pig, and some green Jack-daws,
And a lovely Monkey with lollipop paws,
And forty bottles of Ring-Bo-Ree,
    And no end of Stilton Cheese.
        Far and few, far and few,
        Are the lands where the Jumblies live;
        Their heads are green, and their hands are blue,
        And they went to sea in a Sieve.

And in twenty years they all came back,
  In twenty years or more,
And every one said, 'How tall they've grown!
For they've been to the Lakes, and the Torrible Zone,
  And the hills of the Chankly Bore;'
And they drank their health, and gave them a feast
Of dumplings made of beautiful yeast;
And every one said, 'If we only live,
We too will go to sea in a Sieve, –
  To the hills of the Chankly Bore!'
    Far and few, far and few,
    Are the lands where the Jumblies live;
    Their heads are green, and their hands are blue,
    And they went to sea in a Sieve.

THE PELICAN CHORUS

King and Queen of the Pelicans we;
No other birds so grand we see!
None but we have feet like fins!
With lovely leathery throats and chins!
    Ploffskin, Pluffskin, Pelican jee!
    We think no Birds so happy as we!
    Plumpskin, Ploshkin, Pelican jill!
    We think so then, and we thought so still!

We live on the Nile. The Nile we love.
By night we sleep on the cliffs above;
By day we fish, and at eve we stand
On long bare islands of yellow sand.
And when the sun sinks slowly down
And the great rock walls grow dark and brown,
Where the purple river rolls fast and dim
And the Ivory Ibis starlike skim,
Wing to wing we dance around,—
Stamping our feet with a flumpy sound,—
Opening our mouths as Pelicans ought,
And this is the song we nightly snort;—
    Ploffskin, Pluffskin, Pelican jee!
    We think no Birds so happy as we!
    Plumpskin, Ploshkin, Pelican jill!
    We think so then, and we thought so still!

Last year came out our Daughter, Dell;
And all the Birds received her well.
To do her honour, a feast we made
For every bird that can swim or wade.
Herons and Gulls, and Cormorants black,
Cranes, and Flamingoes with scarlet back,
Plovers and Storks, and Geese in clouds,
Swans and Dilberry Ducks in crowds.
Thousands of Birds in wondrous flight!
They ate and drank and danced all night,
And echoing back from the rocks you heard
Multitude-echoes from Bird and Bird,—
    Ploffskin, Pluffskin, Pelican jee!
    We think no Birds so happy as we!
    Plumpskin, Ploshkin, Pelican jill!
    We think so then, and we thought so still!

Yes, they came; and among the rest,
The King of the Cranes all grandly dressed.
Such a lovely tail! Its feathers float
Between the ends of his blue dress-coat;
With pea-green trowsers all so neat,
And a delicate frill to hide his feet,—
(For though no one speaks of it, every one knows,
He has got no webs between his toes!)

As soon as he saw our Daughter Dell,
In violent love that Crane King fell,—
On seeing her waddling form so fair,
With a wreath of shrimps in her short white hair.
And before the end of the next long day,
Our Dell had given her heart away;
For the King of the Cranes had won that heart,
With a Crocodile's egg and a large fish-tart.
She vowed to marry the King of the Cranes,
Leaving the Nile for stranger plains;
And away they flew in a gathering crowd,
Of endless birds in a lengthening cloud.
  Ploffskin, Pluffskin, Pelican jee!
  We think no Birds so happy as we!
  Plumpskin, Ploshkin, Pelican jill!
  We think so then, and we thought so still!

And far away in the twilight sky,
We heard them singing a lessening cry,—
Farther and farther till out of sight,
And we stood alone in the silent night!
Often since, in the nights of June,
We sit on the sand and watch the moon;—
She has gone to the great Gromboolian plain,
And we probably never shall meet again!
Oft, in the long still nights of June,
We sit on the rocks and watch the moon;—
 —She dwells by the streams of the Chankly Bore,
And we probably never shall see her more.
 Ploffskin, Pluffskin, Pelican jee!
 We think no Birds so happy as we!
 Plumpskin, Ploshkin, Pelican jill!
 We think so then, and we thought so still!

THE POBBLE WHO HAS NO TOES

The Pobble who has no toes
    Had once as many as we;
When they said, 'Some day you may lose them all;'—
    He replied, — 'Fish fiddle de-dee!'
And his Aunt Jobiska made him drink,
Lavender water tinged with pink,
For she said, 'The World in general knows
There's nothing so good for a Pobble's toes!'

The Pobble who has no toes
 Swam across the Bristol Channel;
But before he set out he wrapped his nose,
 In a piece of scarlet flannel.
For his Aunt Jobiska said, 'No harm
Can come to his toes if his nose is warm;
And it's perfectly known that a Pobble's toes
Are safe, — provided he minds his nose.'

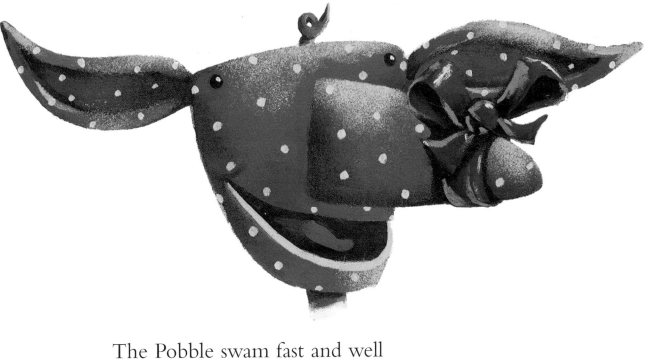

The Pobble swam fast and well
 And when boats or ships came near him
He tinkledy-binkledy-winkled a bell
 So that all the world could hear him.
And all the Sailors and Admirals cried,
When they saw him nearing the further side,—
'He has gone to fish, for his Aunt Jobiska's
Runcible Cat with crimson whiskers!'

But before he touched the shore,
     The shore of the Bristol Channel,
A sea-green Porpoise carried away
     His wrapper of scarlet flannel.
And when he came to observe his feet
Formerly garnished with toes so neat
His face at once became forlorn
On perceiving that all his toes were gone!

And nobody ever knew
    From that dark day to the present,
Whoso had taken the Pobble's toes,
    In a manner so far from pleasant.
Whether the shrimps or crawfish gray,
Or crafty Mermaids stole them away—
Nobody knew; and nobody knows
How the Pobble was robbed of his twice five toes!

The Pobble who has no toes
    Was placed in a friendly Bark,
And they rowed him back, and carried him up,
    To his Aunt Jobiska's Park.
And she made him a feast at his earnest wish
Of eggs and buttercups fried with fish;—
And she said, — 'It's a fact the whole world knows,
That Pobbles are happier without their toes!'

THE QUANGLE WANGLE'S HAT

On the top of the Crumpetty Tree
    The Quangle Wangle sat,
But his face you could not see,
    On account of his Beaver Hat.
For his Hat was a hundred and two feet wide,
With ribbons and bibbons on every side
And bells, and buttons, and loops, and lace,
So that nobody ever could see the face
    Of the Quangle Wangle Quee.

The Quangle Wangle said
    To himself on the Crumpetty Tree,—
'Jam; and jelly; and bread;
    Are the best food for me!
But the longer I live on this Crumpetty Tree
The plainer than ever it seems to me
That very few people come this way
And that life on the whole is far from gay!'
    Said the Quangle Wangle Quee.

But there came to the Crumpetty Tree,
    Mr. and Mrs. Canary;
And they said, — 'Did you ever see
    Any spot so charmingly airy?
May we build a nest on your lovely Hat?
Mr. Quangle Wangle, grant us that!
O please let us come and build a nest
Of whatever material suits you best,
    Mr. Quangle Wangle Quee!'

And besides, to the Crumpetty Tree
    Came the Stork, the Duck, and the Owl,
The Snail, and the Bumble-Bee,
    The Frog, and the Fimble Fowl
(The Fimble Fowl, with a Corkscrew leg);
And all of them said, — 'We humbly beg,
We may build our homes on your lovely Hat,—
Mr. Quangle Wangle, grant us that!
    Mr. Quangle Wangle Quee!'

And the Golden Grouse came there,
    And the Pobble who has no toes,—
And the small Olympian bear,—
    And the Dong with a luminous nose.
And the Blue Baboon, who played the flute,—
And the Orient Calf from the Land of Tute,—
And the Attery Squash, and the Bisky Bat,—
All came and built on the lovely Hat
    Of the Quangle Wangle Quee.

And the Quangle Wangle said
    To himself on the Crumpetty Tree,—
'When all these creatures move
    What a wonderful noise there'll be!'
And at night by the light of the Mulberry moon
They danced to the Flute of the Blue Baboon,
On the broad green leaves of the Crumpetty Tree,
And all were as happy as happy could be,
    With the Quangle Wangle Quee.

The End